Meadowfoam of Oz

Family of Oz series, Volume 4

Josie Ann Tyler

Published by Josie Ann TYler, 2024.

MEADOWFOAM OF OZ

First edition. August 29, 2024.

ISBN: 979-8227197290

Written by Josie Ann Tyler.

Table of Contents

Chapter 1

We woke up to a strange feeling that did not feel quite right. It was different from most days. There was just something in my stomach that didn't feel right.

I tried to go back to sleep, but Tammy's dog would not let me. Reba has to go to the bathroom. Like every morning, Tammy dressed and made her bed before taking the dog out. By the time she came back inside from doing her job. Almost all of the rest of my siblings were up and getting ready to do their chores.

Mom was fixing scrambled eggs, hash browns, and toast. When everyone was done with their chores, breakfast was ready for them to eat. Tammy was standing in the kitchen handing the plates of food to each kid as they came up.

After breakfast, Tammy went to get her dog's leash and got ready to go on a walk. A lot of the time I walked with her so that day I asked her if I could go. Like always she said I had to ask Mom first. I asked Mom and she said that I could. All the rest of the kids wanted to go too so they could wade in the water at the creek that's down the road.

Josie wanted to take her dog with her on the walk so she could play in the water too. Reba hates getting wet. It is like a punishment for her. She is a little Chihuahua that prefers the heat rather than the cold water. Tammy and I

decided to let Josie come along because she could help keep us safe with her bigger dog. (We live in the country where some wild animals could potentially kill us...) She brought her camera with her so that if she saw something to take a picture of she could.

We went down the road and at the curve, just past the hill, there was a large open field. That day in the field there was a herd of elk. It was cool to see them that close instead of as we were driving by going home. Josie was very happy she had brought her camera because she had something to be her subject. She took it out of the case and zoomed in to get a better picture. Just as she was about to snap the picture, Tammy yelled, "Come on, you are holding us up!"

The elk heard the noise and ran away. Josie looked at Tammy with evil eyes and spoke in an angry tone saying, "Thanks a lot for scaring the elk," she said.

"Not my problem. You just weren't fast enough to take the picture," he told her.

We got to the bridge and went down the path that led to the creek that ran underneath the bridge. All of us were having a great time. The dogs, Josie, Tammy, and me. Reba sat on a boulder watching everyone. She went into the water by herself. This was a first for her. She didn't usually do that. Tammy asked Josie if she would take a picture to remember her dog standing in the water. She was still a little mad at me so she just barely took her camera out of her bag and took a picture of Reba. It was kind of funny to see little tiny Reba standing there shivering in the icy water.

On the other side of the bridge, a beaver was building his dam. Josie got out of the water and grabbed her camera. She ran up the bank to where the rest of us had gone to wait for her. We crossed the road to the other side of the bridge. She took her camera out and she got a good shot of the beaver. It was her first time seeing a beaver in the wild. It was the first time for all of us.

After we oohed and ahhed for a while Tammy broke it up by announcing loudly, "We have been here for over 2 hours. We should get back home for lunch."

Everyone came out of the water and dried their selves off in the sun. Because it was summertime we were wearing our flip-flops, so we put them back on. Both dogs shook the water off before climbing up the bank. Suddenly a bright light shone and Darla was being taken up in it and a weird feeling was upon me.

In an instant, I was in the field and it looked like I was really small. I was able to see all the rest of the gang standing there wondering where I had gone. They started yelling at me to come out and to stop hiding.

Tammy was getting nervous, and Josie yelled for me to stop playing around, "It's not funny anymore," she said.

But I still did not show up. They were sure I was still goofing around and thinking it was funny.

Josie ran home with her dog and let Mom and Dad know what was going on. After that, she went and put her dog in her pen.

Mom and Dad were busy trying to get the bull back home after he broke through the fence and went over to the neighbor's yard.

Josie ran over to help them out. "I need to tell you something," she told them when she ran up to them.

Dad looked her way. "Can't you see we are busy right now? You can tell us later when we have the bull back in the pasture."

After some time, they finally got the bull back in the pasture.

"Now, what is so important that you couldn't wait to tell us?" Dad asked.

"We were on our way home when a bright light was shining over the 6 bee boxes down the road. The next thing we knew Darla was nowhere to be seen. We looked for her but could not find her."

Mom and Dad looked at each other and said at the same time, "Here we go again. Another one disappearing into Oz."

"Connie, we might as well go look just in case she was hiding somewhere they didn't think to look," Dad said,

" I guess you are right." Connie looked at her husband. "Who will be the next one missing?"

"I don't think I want to know!"

Josie followed behind, hoping Darla would show up by the time they got to where the others were.

Chapter 2

The kids all ran to Dad and Mom. Tammy was lingering a little ways behind where they stood.

Larry was the first one to speak up, "Tammy is the one that let Darla get lost!"

Mom and Dad both looked at Tammy and they could tell that what Larry had said upset her.

Dad looked at Larry, "It's not Tammy's fault. She didn't know a bright light would cover all of you and make it so that she could not see. It would have happened even if Mom and I were here. How come you weren't watching the little kids, Larry? You're the big brother." Dad asked him.

Larry just stood there without saying a word and they could tell that he felt terrible for what he said.

"Let's take one more look around and see if we can find Darla," Dad said

For the next 10 minutes, they all went looking and calling for Darla but still had no luck.

Dad yelled, "Let's all go home. Maybe she will be there."

They all didn't believe Darla would be home. How could she get past us? They thought.

They went inside and mom told them to go check outside and down by the creek to see if she was anywhere around the farm and was just hiding because she thought it was funny.

Blair yelled to the rest of the kids to make sure that they could all hear her. "If you find her yell at the top of your lungs so that the rest of us can hear you and we can all run to you to make sure she is ok!"

Blair was the oldest, so she decided to go check the creek out. She hoped Darla hadn't drowned. As she walked down the creek, she kept her mouth shut. She kept praying that Darla was safe.

After a while of searching, they all came back to the back porch looking discouraged. They hadn't found Darla anywhere on the farm and that just wasn't normal for her.

Larry just then remembered, " Why are we so worried about Darla?" he paused. The other kids looked at him like he was crazy for even thinking that question.

Larry continued as if they hadn't looked at him like he was a nutcase, "Haven't you guys noticed any similarities to all the disappearances in the family?"

They all sat there thinking of what Larry had just said.

Abigail spoke up, "I guess we all should have put two and two together."

Mom noticed them all just sitting on the back porch. She walked over and opened the sliding glass door. "Did you find Darla?"

Josie turned around and looked at Mom, replying, "No."

"Well, you all better come in and have lunch. Then you all need to clean your room before you can watch a movie and have popcorn."

I looked around. *Where am I?* Then out of the corner of my eyes, I noticed bees, but they did not look like regular bees. They were walking and even talking. I could understand every word that they were saying. *This is pretty creepy, I* thought. And man it sure was hot here.

All of a sudden I hear loud footsteps behind me and then a hand touching my back. The person behind me said in a loud voice, "Don't you move! You are under arrest." They turn me around and I realize that there are two soldier-looking bees and they both grabbed an arm. "Come with us!"

I was so scared I didn't know what would happen to me. "I just want to go home." I tried telling the soldiers. "Silence!" one soldier said. I was so scared by this point that I had tears running down my cheeks.

They pushed a button and the doors opened. It was an elevator. I looked up and saw a bee turning the rope making it move up. Just as I put my head down, the doors opened. I walk out with them. Of course, I kind of had to because I was being held by my arms.

It felt twice as hot up here. I noticed on one door it said Nursery Room and across the hall a sign said Junior Schoolroom. Coming out of the nursery room was a bee in a white dress and a white nurse's hat. There was another door that said Kitchen. On the other side, a sign said Doctor A's office. Another door says Birthing Room. The last door said First Aid Room. We turned to our right and I noticed a vending machine but all they had were cans of honey to drink along with bottles of water.

As we were walking I kept seeing rooms with patients in them. I finally knew where I was. This is a hospital. We turned another corner and two more soldiers were standing in front of a step. Above the step was a sign that said Queen Bee Quarters with an arrow pointing up. As we were standing there we did not know yet what would happen.

Chapter 3

The soldier on the left said, "We need to see the queen. We have a trespasser." One of the soldiers walked over to push a phone button.

I could not tell what the soldier bee was saying. He came back and said, "You may see the queen now."

We strolled up the steps until we came to another door. The soldier on my left rang the doorbell and moments later a bee in a black suit and white tie opened the door.

"Follow me," he told us. My knees were shaking and I felt like I was going to barf at any given moment. We walked into this really big room. It was so big it reminded me of the ballroom in Beauty and the Beast. The throne was straight ahead of us and the queen was sitting on it.

As we got closer to the throne all of the soldiers started to bow. I wasn't sure if I was supposed to bow also.

One of the soldiers kicked me and said in a sharp tone, "You need to bow to the queen bee." So I bowed.

The Queen blinked her eyes and said, "At last, the princess is back."

I turned my head and looked behind me, but I did not see anybody.

THE QUEEN ORDERED THE soldiers to get their hands off the princess. All the while I had no idea what was going on.

The soldiers did not understand what the queen was talking about.

She asked me to come closer. I did as she commanded.

"Don't you know who you are?" She asked me.

"Yes, I'm Darla from Lebanon," I replied.

"No, you are the princess of the Bees in Oz." She told me as if it was the most obvious thing in the world.

The queen could tell I was confused. "Go look at the picture by the door." She pointed at it.

I walked over to the picture and I could not believe my eyes! I'm the picture on the wall was me standing there when I was about 4 years old wearing a tiara. I looked back at the queen. It was such a shock.

"Come sit by me and I will tell you how you became the princess." I went and sat down next to the very nice-looking Queen Bee. "On spring morning a long time ago, while I was still sleeping I was awoken by a noise outside of my castle window. I wanted to find out what it was and so I went to go look. Outside there was a box just sitting there. No one was around and you were the one in the box." She paused.

"I asked my soldiers to bring you into my quarters. I knew you could not live with us because you were a human and would be too tall so I had to use magic to make you small but you would still grow up and live longer than you would in the human world. I adopted you. But one day when you were playing, you opened the door to the outside and disappeared. We never saw you again. Until now." she smiled as she finished the story.

"But I have a family in the outside world with two brothers and three sisters, a mom, and dad who adopted us," I tried telling her.

"Can you tell me more about your life after you left here?" She asked me.

"I was in foster care in Texas, along with my two brothers and my three sisters. They adopted us, and they lived in Lebanon, but our one sister is not blood-related. They adopted her from Poulsbo, Washington."

"So you were taken a long way away."

"I guess my actual parents found me and I moved in with them. That is the only way I know this could have happened" I told the queen. "And I was too young to know anything else"

Chapter 4

"As the queen, I welcome my long-lost daughter back." She clapped her hands and a tall bee came strolling out with a black coat tail on and a white shirt on.

"Please get the princess's tiara and her bee wings." She told the bee.

Before I could say a word, he was back standing in front of me with a tiara and a pair of bee wings on a silver tray. Placing the silver tray on the pillar stand, he took the tiara off, walked over to me, and placed it on my head.

He walked back over to the tray and picked up the bee wings. I was wondering how they would get bee wings to stick on my back and stay.

He came back and placed them on the upper part of my back. I felt something weird happening slowly. It was like the wings were attaching themself to my body

I felt both of the wings and tugged "Ouch!!!!"

Then it just dawned on me. *Did I go to Oz also or am I dreaming?*

I never heard my brothers or sisters talk about bees in Oz. Maybe I'm in another type of adventure story.

Should I ask the queen bee about this? I thought.

I TURNED AROUND AND looked at the queen. "Can I ask you something?"

"Sure." replied the Queen.

"This might sound funny but, am I in Oz?."

The queen looked surprised. I thought to myself, *I must be in Oz. Because she seems surprised I would even ask.*

"Yes, you are in the country of Meadowfoam. We are very close to the Deadly Desert," she answered.

"But what if I want to go back home can't I go see Ozma?"

"It will take weeks to get to Emerald City from here."

"But I could always go on my own."

"No daughter of mine is going to go by herself when she is a princess. Just put it out of your mind and enjoy your life here."

A servant walked in. "Dinner is served," he said.

"Come along Darla, let's eat dinner." the queen implored me.

I was nervous and wondered what food they would serve at the table. They set the table in gold and silver. It was so pretty.

On the table, there were different bugs and honey to dip the bugs in. At first, I was afraid to try the bugs but then I figured it would offend the queen if I didn't. So I made the best of it and just ate them. I pretended it was chicken with

honey on it and drank as much water as I could so it would fill me up and I would be able to eat fewer bugs.

Should I ask the queen bee about this again? I thought I better not.

Chapter 5

I was upset because I thought I would never get to go home and see my brothers, sisters, dad, and mom again.

What would my parents think if I died or would they consider I accidentally went to Oz as my brothers and sisters did?

The butler showed me to my bedroom. They decorated the room with fresh flowers. It was like walking into a flower forest. There were even stuffed animals around the bedroom. The bed looked like a flower.

And in the corner was a sunflower chair and stool.

It was the prettiest bedroom I had ever seen. I wish I could have a bedroom like this back at home. But it would never happen. I have to share a room with my sister.

Back at home, time is different. I remember what my sisters said when they came back. They were at the same place and time when they disappeared.

But we all found my brother in bed. He was not in the same place when he disappeared.

So I'll just have to make the best of it till I find someone to take me to Emerald City and I get to talk to Ozma.

I was so tired. I walked over to the dresser and opened the second drawer and pulled out a pink silk nightgown.

I hoped this would fit me. I took all of my clothes off and folded them. I laid them on the stool that was at the end of my bed.

The nightgown fit me like it was made just for me. Now I needed to find a hairbrush. I looked around the room. There was a wooden vanity, and lying on it was a silver brush, a comb, and a handheld mirror. My grandma had these, and she told me they were antiques.

I was so tired from all of this. I went over to the bed and slipped under the silk sheets, and before I knew it, someone was knocking on the bedroom door and the sun was shining through the curtains.

At first, I forgot where I was. I thought I was home and my younger brother was knocking on my bedroom door like he does a lot in the mornings.

I rolled over and noticed the room was not my room like back home, it was them that I remembered where I was.

Slowly, I got out of bed and went to open the door. Standing in front of me was a lady dressed as you would see in an old Western movie. I think they called them a lady's maid. My sister Abigail said they came in the morning and laid out the clothes you were to wear for that day and helped you get dressed. My sister Abigail said lots of rich people had them in the 1700s and 1800s.

"I DON'T KNOW ABOUT this but let's not be late for breakfast. The queen does not like that," said the ladymaid.

She went over to the wardrobe and picked out the very best-looking dress that had a gorgeous pair of bee wings attached to it.

Because I had never put on a dress like that ever before it took the lady's mad a while to get me into it. When we were done getting me all ready with my hair done and everything, we went down to the dining hall to eat breakfast. It seemed to me that it was taking forever for the Queen to come to the table.

One of the soldiers to my left whispered to me, "We are not allowed to do any talking until the Queen has sat down at the table. Our hands are to stay in our laps at all times until the Queen gives us the order for us to eat and talk."

Because thought it was super dumb I rolled my eyes and said oooh in a sassy way that my mom always hated when I used it.

The soldier just gave me an evil eye.

At that point, I felt out of place.

The Queen looked around to see if everyone was seated at the table before she gave the word, "You may all eat and talk amongst yourselves."

THE QUEEN LOOKED OVER to her right and asked the soldier bee to switch seats with me so that I would be closer to her.

"But I have always sat here ever since I was promoted to Secretary of Defense 2 years ago after Bud died." the soldier complained.

"Are you going to sit there and argue with me or are you just going to move as I ask? If you make me mad I will demote you back to the lowest bee worker in the colony!" she shouted.

Evey Bee had their eyes on the queen and secretary of defense.

With a huff, he got up pushed his chair in, and walked over to me. He waited there until I got up.

I waited a couple of seconds before getting up from my chair.

Through all of this, I was hoping and thinking if there had to be some way that the Queen Bee would let me go to the Emerald City.

The queen kept talking so much that I never thought I would have a chance to speak or get a word in edgewise.

Eventually, I did get a chance to tell her how I felt. I didn't feel like calling her mom so I just decided to say it the way it would sound best to her.

"Your Highness, I appreciate how you took care of me when you found me, but I can not live here. My brothers and sisters are back home waiting for me and I would like

to go to Emerald City and talk to Princess Ozma and see if she can send me home. Even though I would like to go home I would still love to come and visit often." I took a deep breath, and thought to myself, *I'm sure glad I got this off my chest.* I noticed the queen bee did not look so happy at what I said.

"It's a long hard trip to get to Emerald City from here and it will take weeks. We have to take a boat across the Nonestic Ocean and it can be a rough journey.

But if you are that determined, I would have to go and so would my Royal Bee bodyguards. I do not want my daughter to get hurt along the way." The queen tapped her spoon on the water glass twice. Everyone was listening.

"My daughter wants to go back to the other home where she has been. She said she has brothers and sisters there and she misses them. I haven't used my palanquin in a very long time. It will take us 3 days to fix it up and make sure there are no tears and that the seat will be comfortable."

"So is it like an automobile?" I asked.

The queen looked at me and replied "No, a palanquin is where we sit in with a cover over our head to keep the sun off each of us and there will be 4 soldiers one on each corner hanging on to the metal rod that has a cover over the rod so it will not get so hot that the soldiers can not touch it." she continued talking as if I hadn't just interrupted her. "I will have to contact my cartographer before we go on the trip."

I felt like an idiot for asking questions so much but I didn't know what a cartographer was. So I decided to ask the queen. "What is a cartographer?" I asked.

"It is a person who draws maps and knows the land. He will help us find the right route to take on a trip.

I thought for a moment, "So it's like a GPS?" I asked her after thinking. The queen didn't understand what I was talking about.

"What is a GPS?" she asked me.

"My dad told me a GPS is an electronic map that is done on computers instead of using paper to make a map. You use it in your automobile and you type the address in and it speaks to you and tells you where to turn and how far away you are from the places."

It was so quiet. I looked around and everyone at the table was looking at me. It gave me the willies."

It seemed like time stood still at that very moment.

Chapter 6

Just as I took my last bite of food, in a soft voice the queen said "You have school today."

I thought to myself *what would school be like here?* "What kind of school is here?" I asked.

The queen turned and looked over at her guard. "Will you escort the Princess to her school room?"

I stood up and thanked the queen for an excellent breakfast even though I didn't mean it. I was just trying to be polite. My mom taught me to be polite even in circumstances where I hated the actual thing.

When I came into the classroom the guard introduced me to the teacher.

"Nice to have you in our class. You make take the second seat to your left." Before I could sit down she handed me a piece of paper.

When I sat down I read what the paper said.

PRINCESS STUDY

You will be learning these things:

Embroidery, knitting, music, math, English, writing, history, reading, geography, spelling, and foreign language, you will learn 8 different languages how to manage a large household, and how to dress properly. Then after you finish this, on to finishing school!

I knew right then that it was going to be a long day. After what seemed like an eternity of school I was able to be free for a while and then eat dinner and bedhead.

I woke up one morning and realized it had been a month since the queen said we would leave to travel to Emerald City. *Maybe I will never get to go home and see my family again.* I just felt like crying.

The lady maid always picked out what I was going to wear for the day and it was bugging me because I liked to pick out what I wanted to wear.

This morning I was late for breakfast and that was the first time it happened to me.

I walked into the room like I was a dog with my tail on between my back legs. I was pretty scared to see what happened.

In a harsh tone, the queen said, "Take your seat so we can finish eating young lady and I will deal with you later!"

I took my seat as I was ordered. I did not know what was going to happen later. Coming up behind me was the butler with a bowl of corn grits that had honey on top. A glass of water was on the right side of the dish. I thought, *at least this is something I enjoy eating.*

I was quiet during the meal and was just thinking to myself about how I could get out of there and go back home.

But every door to go outside or come in has two security cop bees inside and outside guarding the entrance.

So there is no way for me to leave.

After everyone left the table it was just the queen and me sitting at the table. We sat in silence for a while before the queen spoke.

"I never want you to be late for any meal again, do you understand me?!"

"But the lady that picks out my clothes in the morning was late and I thought I was to always wait to tell her to come."

"Oh, I see well if she is not on time just pick something out to wear and tell me she did not show up." the queen answered.

"I understand now," I said.

"You may go now." she dismissed me with a shoo of her hand.

After school, I had time to go to my room before dinner. I was sitting on a window ledge looking out the window and all of a sudden I saw Josie walking by with her dog. I opened the window and I was yelling "Josie it is me! Help me please!"

She might be able to hear me. I never thought of this before. I thought *I'd jump out the window and run to her.*

Just as I lifted my one leg over the window ledge the siren went off and before I knew it a security bee cop was running into my bedroom.

He grabbed me and pulled me back inside.

The short bee asked me, "What do you think you were doing?"

"I saw my sister walking by and just wanted to go to her but she didn't hear me." I tried explaining.

"Of course, she can't hear you. Human ears are not tuned in to our voices. We talk in a different tone and you are one of us now."

The other bee looked at me and spoke in a sharp tone. "We have security alarms on all windows so nothing can enter our bee hive and destroy it or kill us, but you can open the window for fresh air only," he answered and I could tell he I was a silly little girl.

They turned and left me glancing out the window with tears running down my cheeks.

All I could do was look out the window and watch for my sister to come walking by on the road.

Just then I saw her again. I decided to try it again, "Josie it's me!" I yelled more than once but she never turned around to see who was yelling her name. Her dog was pulling her toward the beehive and Josie yelled at her dog to heel. She did what she told her to do but she still looked back at the beehive as if she wanted to go over to me.

Chapter 7

After putting her dog back in her kennel, Josie walked toward the house to find her mom. When she got a little closer, she could hear the time of her voice. She was upset. She was mad at Frederick for touching her sewing machine again and this time he broke the take-up lever and the tension control.

"Well, what do you have to say for yourself!" Mom asked him.

Fredrick didn't know what to say; he just stood there looking at Mom.

"You can just go to your room and stay in there. I'm gonna go and tell your dad about it and see if he can fix it." She was pretty mad. Frederick was always touching things that weren't his.

Mom got up and put her coat and boots on and went outside to talk to Dad. The kids all ran to the front window but they couldn't make out what they were saying.

They saw them walking back when Dad got in the house. Dad told Frederick to go to the bathroom. "You are going to get a spanking." When they both came back out they could not believe what mom said.

"Fredrick, if you ever get to go to Oz they will never let you come back because you touch and break too many things!"

They all looked at each other. Larry spoke in a quiet voice "Mom's starting to believe more in Oz than we thought she would ever believe in it." He looked amazed.

"Josie, can you come here," Mom asked.

"Be right there Mom.

"Did you see any sight of Darla when you were on your walk?"

"No, but Rusty was acting weird on our walk back. She kept pulling towards the field of meadowfoam."

"Maybe he heard Darla's cat out there, we were looking everywhere for that cat."

"Could be, mom. I'm going to go back and finish my math homework." Josie said.

"Sounds like a good plan to me."

But it was hard to study when your brothers and sister kept coming to her room to talk.

All of this was at the house. At the castle, I noticed it was getting close to dinner and didn't want the queen to yell at me again, so I made sure I left 5 minutes early. But as I walked into the dining room others were there earlier than me.

Just as I took my place at the table the queen entered and took her seat at the head of the table. The butler put a bowl of tomato soup in front of me. I would have never guessed bees would be eating this. I'm glad it was not bugs. I shouldn't have spoken so soon. He places a big bowl of mealworms in the middle of the table.

Well, I should get my fill of soup so I will not have to eat any mealworms. A short time later the dish of mealworms was passed to me. I took the bowl and tried to pass it to the Queen but she wouldn't take the dish.

"You take yours first."

So I took one spoonful before I told her I was full of soup.

"You will eat what's on your plate before you leave," she told me.

I didn't say a word. I just took my fork and started eating. My brothers and sisters would think I was weird for eating bugs.

But if I didn't do what I was told I don't know what would happen to me, so I had to eat the same way all the bees ate or I would go hungry.

The month went into years and before I knew it, I was 14. It was hard to believe I was that old now.

As I was getting ready for bed I was thinking about what I had to do. I thought *I needed to tell the queen that I needed to go whether she liked it or not.*

As I lay in bed I was thinking of ways I could get home. *If I could only get out of the castle, I could go to the road and see if I can get Josie's attention whenever she walks by. Why would I need to go to The Emerald City just to get home?*

The next day after breakfast I waited until everyone left the table before I told the queen what I was going to do.

"You can't just walk home, you can not get there this way."

"I don't understand. I saw my sister walk by when I was in my room." I tried telling her.

"Let me explain something to you. You can only go so far from the beehive that if you make it up to the road there is a clear sheet of glass. You can't go through it without Ozma giving you the okay to go back home. Having this sheet of glass keeps us safe, from humans and other animals."

"But how come all the other bees can go across the street if a glass sheet protects us?

"Because you were not born a working bee and have the powers to go through the glass sheet to go to other plants and bring honey back."

"But you told me years ago in 3 days we would be leaving for The Emerald City and it has not happened yet,"

The queen felt sad because she did not want to lose me again. But deep down she knew she couldn't hold on to me for another day.

The very next day just as the queen said many years ago, she stepped out on the balcony. The trumpets blew and everyone stopped what they were doing and came closer to the castle. "My adopted daughter Princess Darla wants to go back to the human life she had before. So in my absence, I will leave my daughter Dandelion in charge until the time I come back. We have to go to The Emerald City to see Ozma so she can send her back home safely. Behave like you would if I was still here ruling over you. You are in good hands with Dandelion and I know she will do the best she can in my absence." She looked very regal standing there address-ing her people.

The queen waved goodbye and walked back inside. About an hour later the queen and her servants walked out the front door. Darla and the queen got into the palanquin and one of the lady bees covered both the Queen's and Darl's legs with a blanket.

The whole hive waved and said their goodbyes, they all watched until they could not see them anymore.

Chapter 8

On the first day away from the beehive everything went smoothly, nothing bad happened.

"Can I walk for a while?" Darla asks.

"Why?" the queen asked.

"My butt is getting tired of just sitting here. I need to move my legs too." I told her. Maybe using the word butt want the best course of action but it worked well enough.

"Stop!" ordered the queen. The servants placed the palanquin on the ground and I got out of the palanquin and started to walk but before she could go far, the queen told her to stop. "You need to have a servant walk by your side. Remember you are a princess and will always be one even if you are in the human world."

"But I do want to come back and visit. I don't know how I can come back when I never knew how I got here in the first place." I said.

"Ozma will know how to have you come back. Let's not worry over it yet," she said softly.

I walked so much the second day that by night time I was too tired to walk anymore.

"I want to get back in and sit down. I'm tired of walking."

Once again the servants placed the palanquin on the ground and I got back in.

The major servant spoke up, "We will stop in a little while and make camp for the night."

I heard a creek ahead of us and the major servant said, "Let's make camp here for the night and the cook can start dinner before we all turn in for the night,"

I was handed my plate and to my surprise, it was a snail.

"UGH!!! I can't eat this!" I exclaimed

The queen looked up at me. "You will eat what is in front of you or you will just turn around and go back to the beehive. Do I make myself clear?" she said sternly.

"Yes," I replied.

"Go ahead and eat."

"How do you get the snail out?" I asked her.

The queen told me, "We call this escargot not snail. It sounds a lot better than saying snail. Here let me show you how to get the snail out. Take your tongs and hold the shell then use the small snail fork to dig the snail out of the shell. Then dip it in butter and eat it." She demonstrated.

The first time I had trouble getting the snail out of the shell but on the second try I did it before I put it in my mouth I put it up to my nose and smelled it, it didn't have much of a smell. Slowly I put the snail in my mouth and to my surprise, it tasted like mushroom Yum."

"Well, what do you think?"

"It is good. My family will never believe me when I tell them I eat snails, I mean escargot."

"Finish up so we can get some sleep."

I was the first one to wake up. The sun was out already and the birds were singing, ahead of us was a herd of elk.

Before long the queen woke up "Can I ask you something?"

"Why sure."

"We go by this way in the car while we are still in Lebanon."

"Yes, just for a short time we have to get to the stump up ahead then we get to go into Oz you will find out soon enough."

It took us most of the day before we got to the stump once we reached it. A bee guard was standing in front of the stump, "How can

I help you?" The head servant said we need to get to Emerald City. Because Darl wants to go back to the Human world."

"Oh I see one of them again." the Bee guard replied,

"What the holdup?" the queen asked

"Is that the queen bee of Meadowfoam?" Bee Guard asked.

"Yes, sir it is."

"Well, that's different." He left his post to walk over to meet the queen. "Your Majesty." as he bowed.

"You may rise."

"Why don't you camp here for the night and make a fresh start in the morning,"

The queen spoke loud so everyone would hear her. "We will be camping here for the night. We will wake up at 6:30, eat breakfast, and then be on our way."

Chapter 9

The next thing I noticed we were moving again up the stump. It scared me. I thought I would fall out of the palanquin. I was lucky I didn't. We made it to the top of the stump. One thing I could not figure out was how come everyone except the queen and I had to walk around the top of the stump seven times.

Then all of a sudden the stump opened. I saw steps going down the stump. My heart was beating a mile a minute. I thought I was going to have a heart attack and die. It was so warm and damp down here, I was sweating like a pig.

As we were coming down the steps I could see millions of stink bugs all over the place. I looked at the queen and said, "I'm glad I don't have to walk. I would not want to step on any of those stink bugs. I would smell so bad." I scrunched my nose in disgust.

The queen looked around and then back at me. "Didn't you know that you have to eat them at dinner?" she asked me.

"Ugh!!" I replied.

"We get them when they die and they are delivered to the beehive."

After she told me this I just sat on the palanquin for a while and couldn't stop thinking about the fact that I had usually eaten the bugs.

The queen ordered the soldiers holding us to stop walking around and around before we disturbed the bugs too much.

I decided to cover my whole body and lay down and take a nap till we got out of there. This didn't bother the queen one bit she just stayed awake and looked around.

The stink bugs didn't bother us after they saw it was the queen bee coming. It took us most of the day to get out of the stump. It was bigger than I thought. I woke back up and noticed we were still in the stump. Up ahead I could see a crack with light shining through.

Slowly we all made it safely out of the stump and into the bright sunlight. Part of the reason it was so bright was because right outside of the stump was the yellow brick road. It was so bright. Much brighter than in the movie.

I could smell grapefruit on both sides of the yellow brick road. There were grapefruit trees as far as my eyes could see.

Mom would like to visit these places because she loves grapefruit. We kept going until we came to a sign that said

Welcome to Grapefruit Village.

As we entered the village I noticed that the people were dressed in the same color as a grapefruit. The whole town smelled of grapefruit. The people just stood around looking at us and talking and pointing as we kept walking through the town. There were names by the business but I could not understand what they said. I did not know the language.

It was getting late and we had to find a place to sleep. "Up ahead is an inn by the looks of it," the queen said. As we approached the inn the front guard walked inside to ask if there were any available rooms for the night.

In the next couple of minutes, he came back and let the queen know. "There are only two available rooms, one for you and one for the princess. The man behind the desk said the rest of us could sleep in the field out back. Breakfast would be served to both parties." He told her.

The queen went in first. I followed her. The bellboy showed us each room. We were across from each other. I thought my room was not a bad place to sleep, but it had a little too much orange for a room this size. At least in my opinion.

It reminded me of all the times that Tammy would talk about the style of the 70s. I guess they used to paint their walls orange.

As soon as I got into bed I fell fast asleep and didn't wake up once until I heard a knock on the door.

I was so warm under the comforter that I didn't care who was knocking on the door I turned over and tried to go back to sleep but I heard the knock once again.

Then a voice said that I needed to get up for breakfast. "I have your dress picked out for you to wear."

That was when I knew who it was. It was my lady's maid. I jumped out of my bed and started to get dressed. I didn't want to be late and have the queen mad at me again for being late to a meal.

I was so happy that breakfast was not bugs again. I should have known that they would serve grapefruit for breakfast. Which they did. Along with eggs, hash browns, toast, and tea.

We thanked the manager and then we were out the door. Standing in front of the inn was the palanquin waiting for us.

After we got comfortable, the servant girl came and placed the blankets over our legs. Then off we went. It made me think of being in a parade.

Up ahead was a line of kids. At the front of the line was an adult who must have been their teacher. She turned around and spoke in a language I didn't know. As we came by, all the kids and the teacher bowed.

"Why did they bow to you?" I asked.

"Because I'm a queen."

"But you are not their queen and anyway, how did they know you are a queen?"

"They saw my crown." She smiled after saying that because I think she thought that my question was a little silly. "And no, I'm not their queen but in this town, they teach their children to respect royalty," she told me.

"But when we first came into the town I didn't see anybody bow."

"There were some that did out of respect but most didn't because I'm not their queen," she replied.

"I understand now," I said. As we approached the end of the town I saw a skateboard park and it wasn't just children and teenagers skateboarding, there were adults as well.

We all turned around and took our last look at this interesting town.

Chapter 10

Here we were again. More trees this time, but these trees were all maple trees. Something was different about these maple trees. They each had a spout with a bucket next to the tree, and stuff was coming out slowly.

"How come these trees have spouts and are dripping some liquid into a bucket?" I asked the queen.

The queen couldn't help but chuckle, then it turned into a laugh. Soon enough she was laughing so hard she had tears running down her face.

"What's so funny?" I asked, very confused.

Finally, the queen stopped laughing. She took a deep breath, "Haven't you ever seen a maple tree give out sap before?" I shook my head no. "That's a part of how they make maple syrup. And then when the buckets are full of the sap they take it back to the factory and finish cooking up the syrup.

"Not where I live. So is this a maple tree farm?"

"Yes," she answered.

"Maybe they have this type of farm in other states that I don't know of." I pondered aloud.

"Could be." the queen said.

A couple hours later I looked ahead and saw what looked to me like a factory. As we got closer there were 2 other brick roads. To our left was a brown brick road and to our right was a yellow brick road.

"Let's take the brown brick road," I suggested.

"The yellow brick road takes you to Emerald City, not the brown brick road." The queen replied.

This kind of upset me. There could be a way down the brown road that gets us to Emerald City faster than the yellow brick road could. And I voiced that opinion to the queen.

A guy was standing by his car in the factory parking lot and he overheard our conversation. He walked over to us. "I wouldn't go down that brown brick road if you paid me."

"Why?" I asked him.

"I better not say anything. I don't want something to happen to me and my family." He answered.

With a whiny voice, I said. "But I need to know now!"

The man got tired of hearing my whining and he said, "Oh shut up and stop whining!"

One of the servants stopped the palanquin completely and turned to the queen. "Madame, if I may speak?"

"You may."

"There is a sign here that says there is a tour at the factory. It might be a good idea to go there for a while." HE suggested.

"Sounds like a good plan, maybe this will make Darla shut up and think better." She replied as she looked at me with an annoyed expression.

I just smirked because all I wanted was to get out of the palanquin.

We got out of the palanquin. The bee carriers put the palanquin under the steps hoping nobody would take it.

We got there just in time for the last free tour of the year.

The lady behind the desk asked us all to sign in and where we were from. We all signed our names,

We had a guy take us on the tour but before we went he spoke first." The sap of a sugar maple tree is 98 percent water and 2 percent sugar and it is that 2 percent that will yield a delicious sweetener. It takes 40 gallons of sap to make 1 gallon of syrup. It is simply by boiling the sap to remove water and thus concentrate the sugar that makes maple syrup follow me."

We walked down a long hallway then through a double door there were glass windows and we could see people in the room they had nets covering their hair, long white coats, and plastic gloves on.

"Here are the five steps involved from start to finish:

1. Preparing for the season;

2 . Determining when to do it at the right time.

3. Identifying the trees to be tapped and tapped

4. Collecting the sap and processing (boiling/evaporating) it.

5. Filtering, grading, and packing the syrup.

We walked down the hall and turned to our left another room with big windows.

The tour guide told us "This is where maple butter is made and they always use a brass mixer. First, they have to put cream in a stand mixer start by adding 6 cups of chilled

heavy cream to the bowl of a stand mixer fitted with a whisk attachment.

In the second step, beat the cream well. The third step strains out the buttermilk. The fourth step is to add the salt and mix again for 45 seconds then two men will carry the butter over to the table and pour it into the butter container. We always triple the butter making. Next, I will take you to where they make Maple Cookies. This will be the last place on the tour."

I was getting hungry but I kept on going hoping they would give me a cookie as we watched how they were made.

We just stood there watching as they made the cookie batter.

"Remember a good maple cookie is made with real butter and dark brown sugar, also real maple syrup and real vanilla extract, no imitation vanilla extract."

Darla tapped the tour guide on his shoulder and he turned and looked at me.

"What is the other part of the room for?"

"That's where they make the maple glaze for the top of the cookie and they roast pecans and fry bacon. They will crumble the bacon on the cookie with chopped pecans. All cookies are in the shape of leaves."

We watched for some time before the tour guide said anything more.

"Follow me back out."

When we got back to the front desk the lady looked at us, "You may step over here and take two cookies and a cup of water, and thank you for coming into the day."

Chapter 11

As we came out two children were playing in the palanquin with their dolls. Darla walked up to them. You are going to have to get out of the palanquin. We need to use this for the queen and me.

They would not move. I repeated it but they still ignored me.

A short plump red-haired lady comes up to me. "I see you are having trouble getting the kids to move."

She turned her head and looked at the kids and was talking to them in a language I did not understand.

They both grabbed their doll and went down the yellow brick road.

"Thanks for helping me out."

"You are welcome."

The four walking bee servants each picked up the handle and brought it out from under the step. The queen climbed in first.

Darl started whining once again "I still want to go down the brown brick road."

The Queen was so tired of Darla whining that she finally gave in and all the servants just looked at the queen and couldn't believe she gave in.

"LET'S AMUSE HER AND just go down the brown brick road and she will see there is no yellow brick road."

The Queen gave an order there was not much more anybody could say.

Slowly we headed to the brown brick road with all the servants looking back at the yellow brick road before everyone crossed over to the brown brick road.

As we went along it was quiet, not even a bird was chirping.

"Where is everyone?"

The queen didn't say anything because she wasn't sure what to say.

I asked the queen once again but she still didn't respond, I was wondering what was going on that she would not answer me.

It was weird not having any noise around. Now I know how deaf people must feel that went deaf later in life but could hear at one time.

We came up a steep hill. Maybe there will be something over the hill that will say go this way to Emerald City. As we came to the top of the hill I looked around but all I saw were evergreen trees as far as my eyes could see.

The head servant turned around and everyone stopped.

"We need to find places to sleep and make dinner before it gets dark. There was a nice field that had a river running through it.

The river was plentiful with fish jumping in and out of the water.

Darla was getting antsy and whiny "I want to go fishing so I can help bring dinner back."

Now the queen just had about enough of her whinny. "No princess is going fishing, that's what we have servants for!

I thought I was thinking this to myself but I was wrong I said it out loud. "Being a princess is boring."

The queen yelled, "That's enough now I don't want to hear you speak tomorrow."

The servant came with our plates I had never seen a fish with teeth like this, the servant whispered to me, "It's a piranha they don't taste that bad it's like eating cod some people and bees like to eat the head and there is a recipe for piranha soup you just cook the head."

"That's enough you may leave us to eat." The queen said.

I didn't want to fight with the queen so I just ate every part of the piranha. The worst was eating the head. Sure if there was a cat around I would have given it to the cat.

Chapter 12

It has been more than a couple of days and we have not seen anybody since we left the factory.

Darla was sitting on the bank of the river with her feet in the water along with the other servants.

Coming over the grassy hillside were two teenage boys who looked like a beanpole.

Wearing brown bib overalls, their hair reminded me of Alfalfa from the movie The Rascals.

Once they saw us they were scared like Jack rabbits they ran to the close tree and hid behind it.

I couldn't understand why they would be scared of us because we didn't do anything to them.

I looked over at one of the servants and asked. "Should one of us go up there and talk to them and them now we will not hurt them."

"By all means, if that is what you want to do."

I got up leaving my shoes and socks behind and walked slowly up to them, they were shaking and started to leave."

"Please stop, I'm not going to hurt you, I just want to talk to you and get to know you."

They turned around and just stood there saying nothing for the longest time.

The one with light brown hair spoke first. "Who are you?"

"I'M PRINCESS DARLA."

They both were shocked, I guess they never heard of me before and had seen bees dressed up.

"Would you both like to join us at the river? I see you have your fishing poles with you?"

They both looked at each other first before the same boy spoke up. "I guess it will not hurt."

All three walked back to the river, the boys sat by me and were gazing at everyone.

"I forgot to ask your name."

The light brown hair boy replied. "Sam"

The other boy stuttered Rockyy,"

We all said, "Nice to meet you,"

I told them everything that happened to me and they were surprised.

"I heard the brown brick road was not a very good place to be, that's what the guy told us outside the maple factory. On two different brick roads, one was the yellow brick road and the other was the brown brick road, I thought going this way we might get to Emerald City faster."

Rocky gave her a funny look, "Why would you think this?"

"Because my brother and sister been to Oz and went to the Emerald City too and it took them a long while to get there because they went to lots of different parts before they got to Emerald City

THE SMALLEST BEE SERVANTS asked them, "So what part of Oz are we in."

The light brown hair boy replied. "In a couple of hours, you will be in Cougarville. We live on the outskirts of Cougarville. You will find cougars walking just like humans do and they can talk just like the cowardly lion. Some people are living among them too."

"Are they friendly?" Darla asked.

"It depends, some are and some are not."

Before long the queen approached us in a soft tone I had not heard since the day I first came to the beehive.

"We must be on our way if we are ever going to get to Emerald City."

"Do we have to?" Darla asked "I was having a good time talking to the two boys."

The Queen was upset that Darla was whinnying again.

"You were the one that wanted to go back home and traipse all over the country just to get to Emerald City, and then you would not listen, you had to have it your way by going down the brown brick road when I told you we needed to go the other way. The yellow brick road would have taken us there faster! No more dawdling

I said my goodbyes and followed the queen to the Palanquin.

Nobody said anything for a very long time, and we all heard lots of noise, up ahead was a sign but I could not make out

what it said because I was too far away, one of the servants said we are coming to Cougarville Everyone stopped and died in their tracks, I was scared of cougars I took the blanket and covered my head.

"Would you be so kind as to uncover your head."?The Queen said.

I pulled the blanket off my head and placed it back on my legs.

"Now why did you do that?"

"We have cougars where I live and one day they came after my sister Jose and she had to be taken to the hospital she almost died."

"Sorry to hear this but we do not know they might be very friendly here,"

I shut my eyes as we entered the town. I heard a loud popping sound. My eyes popped open to see what it was but it was just cubs playing with snaps that you dropped on the ground and they popped.

Chapter 13

This town smelled fishy. There were so many seafood grocery stores, and seafood restaurants no wonder the town smelled fishy.

It was strange to me to see cougars dress as humans do.

Every time we went by a cougar they looked at us oddly like we were aliens.

Coming towards us was a taxi bike stopped right by The Queen "I'm Mayor Kenndy and who might you be?"

"I'm The Queen of Meadowfoam and this is Princess Darla."

"We haven't had anybody come to our town in years, would you all like to have dinner at my daughter's restaurant?"

"Thank you, that would be nice." The Queen replied.

"Follow me."

The Taxi bike had to go around the back side of the palanquin to get up front so we all could follow.

As we entered the restaurant there was a large chocolate-flowing fountain with a table of food on each side of the fountain.

"Hi, Dad, what brings you here?"

"We need the best table in the house for The Queen, and Princess and a table for the servants who will not be sitting with us."

"I can put them by the back door. There's a table big enough for them to sit around, Lucy can show the servants to the table by the back door and Dad will order for them.

We followed the Mayor's daughter to the back of the room and up the steps. There was one table only, And it overlooked the whole restaurant.

The Mayor did the ordering "You can get the servants' codfish soup along with spinach salad, rolls, and water to drink.

His daughter told us to follow her, she took us to the back of the restaurant, and up the steps, there was only one table but when you sat down you could see the whole restaurant from up there.

The Mayor ordered, "We will have your special octopus, eel, and crawdads along with chocolate-covered fruit, and sparkling cider for all 3 of us."

I watch one of the waitresses deep in each fruit in the chocolate fountain and place them on a long plate. After she finished she placed the plate on the tray and carried it with one hand up in the air. She walked slowly to the back of the restaurant and up the steps.

"I COULDN'T CARRY THE tray of fruit. I would fall down the step and the fruit would be all over me.

Both The Queen and Mayor softly laughed at what I said. Right after she placed the fruit on table 2 another waitress started up the steps carrying the food and placed the plates in front of us. I will be back with the Mayor's food. Then we had one of the waitresses bring up the sparkling cider and fill our glasses up. Then she put the bottle in the ice bucket.

"Will there be anything else?"

"No" the Mayor replied

The other waitress had a basket full of rolls on the table.

"Can finish what you were saying early," Mayor said.

"Well I found my daughter outside when she was a baby she's human as you can tell, then when she was a toddler I gave her magic bee wings and had to shrink her down to the size of a bee so she could live in the beehive, then one day she got out of the beehive and I didn't see her till she was 8 years old a couple of weeks went by and she wanted to go back to her human life, I told her in 3 days we could go to the Emerald City but first I need to get the palanquin fix but I did not keep my promise, she 14 years old now."

"I understand how you feel she is still your daughter, and it hurts to see her go again.

"May I say something"

"Go ahead? Darla" the Mayor replied

"You see I was walking with my brother and sisters heading back home and this bright light covered us all and the next thing I knew I was in a beehive and very small and these two bee security cops grabbed me and took me to see the Queen when she saw me she had a surprised look on her face, and she told me to go look at the picture on the wall and the picture was me when I was a toddler, then she had them bring me bee wings and they place them on me that why I still have them on, couple week letter I saw my sister and try to go out the window to get to her but the alarm went off, the queen told me you can't get to the road because there an invisible glass there, I ask her then why can the bee get by, she said they have a special power that why we are going Ozma so she can help me get back home and also see if I can come back for visit anytime I want."

"Darla you would be welcome back anytime and your bedroom will be there for you the same way it looks now and I will miss you when you are not here."

It was quiet as they were eating until Darla spoke up.

"How come farmers can go through the glass if I can't?"

"It's because the farmer is special and their helpers on the farm are special just like the bees." The Queen replied.

"THIS IS SOMETHING I will remember for the rest of my life being in a restaurant like this," Darla said.

"I'm glad you enjoyed yourself." The Mayor said.

One of the waitresses returned and asked "Is there anything else you need?"

"No," the Mayor replied.

"Well, we need to be on our way. We both had a wonderful time."

As we went outside the restaurant it was raining hard.

"Oh no we are going to be wet," Darla said.

"No, we will not have a covering over our head, only the servants will. The Queen said.

It was late and I was tired and didn't care so I took my blanket and the pillow and laid down to go to sleep, not much to see when it's dark out anyway.

The queen had the same Idea she decided to go to sleep too.

The servants couldn't go to sleep yet because they needed to keep walking and tell they found a spot to camp overnight.

Chapter 14

I awoke to the servants still carrying the Palanquin. The Queen was still asleep.

I just sat up trying not to wake The Queen but a couple of minutes later The Queen woke up.

She was surprised to see the servants still caring about the Palanquin, after she sat up she took a deep breath and then spoke up "Please stop!"

In an instant, all servants stopped. And they all turn to look at her.

In a loud voice, she spoke so everyone could hear her,

"Why did you guys not find a place to sleep last night?"

The short servant looked at The Queen "Every time we tried someone asked us to get up and move on so we keep moving on all night."

"Oh" replied The Queen

Along about then, we saw a swarm of wasps flying over our heads.

Darla looked over at The Queen "That is the one thing I'm terrified of being stung every spring and summer more than once by a wasp."

"I can see why you are scared, just cover your whole body with your blanket and I will let you know when it's safe to come out from under the blanket."

I DID WHAT THE QUEEN told me to do, it was hot under the blanket and I couldn't wait to get out from underneath it.

Eventually, The Queen told me I could uncover but when I did another swarm of wasps came and they were bigger than the last swarm of wasps.

I grabbed that blanket fast and covered it up again under the blanket. The queen could hear me crying. I was wishing my mom was here to hold me.

I don't like this part of Oz is not a nice place. I just want to get out of this place now and go back home. I kept saying this over and over again hoping it would come true but no luck.

I slowly lowered the blanket down as soon as I did there was a wasp right in front of me, I covered myself back up but I still could hear the buzzing sound of the wasp,

I wish I was deaf like Tammy.

I didn't know I said that out loud. The Queen spoke to me in a harsh voice.

"Darla How could you say you wish you were deaf!"

I pulled the blanket down and looked The Queen in the eyes. Before I had time to say anything, The Queen wasps were standing looking at The Queen bee.

In a sarcastic voice"Why are you in my country of Waspville?" The Queen wasps replied.

THE QUEEN BEE TOOK a deep breath before speaking. "I'm trying to get my daughter Darla back home to her family so we need to go to the Emerald City and see if Ozma can help her out."

The wasp queen had a strange look she did not understand. "How can a bee have a human daughter?"

The Queen bee said to herself here I go again to explain about my daughter.

By the time the Queen Bee finished telling her story about her daughter, the Queen wasp looked at me like I flew off my rocker.

"You are nutty as a fruitcake, why did you take the brown brick road the Emerald City takes you there faster?"

"So you mean we can still get to Emerald City on the brown brick road?" The Queen bee asked.

"You will be slow as a turtle getting there this way, too many things will get in your way before you get there."

With a wave of her hand, the swarm of wasps left without giving any other information.

Chapter 15

Back at home, everyone was still looking for Darla every day, but still, no luck.

Fredrick just stood around with a smirk on his face.

"Why are you looking this way?" Larry asked

Jose was sitting on the couch listening to all of them talk about Darla, she was getting tired of it she got up and went into the kitchen.

"Would you all shut up and listen to me? Use your brain to look at what happened to Larry, and Abagail, when you could not find them where did they go?

Everyone remembered and said at the same time "Oz."

Connie came out of her bedroom "Josie stop yelling at your sisters and brothers, what going on? "

Jose turned around and looked at her mom "They were yelling and talking about how Darla and the different ways she disappeared and would not shut up and I was trying to do my homework which they would go do theirs so I can think."

"Okay, let's not talk about this anymore today, You all go do your homework and stay doing it till I come back out of my bedroom.

"Ha! Ha! You all have to do your homework. I'm going outside. "To play," Frederick said.

Connie turns around and looks at Frederick. "Didn't you hear what I just said go do your homework?"

"But I can't!"

"Why not!"

"You never gave me a workbook. I haven't had one for a year."

"Why did you not tell me!"

"I did it more than once!"

All the other children said, "He did Mom."

Connie walked into her bedroom and came back out with a big workbook.

She walked back into her bedroom and slammed the door.

All the older children went into the living room and started on their home, except Friendrick.

Larry looked at the clock on the wall. "We've been doing homework for 3 hours!"

"It can't be that long," Blair said.

Larry yelled, "I know how to tell time!"

Blair looked up at the clock "Oh" but never said sorry for not believing Larry.

Chapter 16

Back in Oz, it has been days since we saw anybody or animals. All we saw were fields and fields of red clover.

Just as I was thinking we should turn back around and try going down the yellow brick road, I heard water flowing just around the corner and I saw the river.

There was a swing bridge over the water. I didn't want to cross that bridge because it was too high up and if I fell I would be killed by the big boulders.

I looked at the queen "Can't we just go around the river I do not want to cross a swing bridge I'm afraid of swing bridges since my brother Larry made the swing bridge we were on the move too much and it was swaying back and forth and I almost fell off it bridge if I did not grab hold of the rope and Abagalia help me get back up I would have been a goner.

"You will be safe. We are inside the Palanquin. If you don't want to look when we cross the swing bridge just lay down and cover your head and go to sleep!

I did what the queen told me slowly the servant carried us across the wind, started picking up and the swing bridge started moving. It felt like it was moving more than when Larry made it move on purpose.

ALL OF A SUDDEN THE servants dropped the Palanquin and it rolled on its side. I crawled out and grabbed hold of the rope and stood up, The rope Bridge was still swaying but not as bad as it was.

Queen Holler "Pick up the Palanquin now and let's get off this bridge at once!"

After they picked it up I got back in and laid down and covered up once again.

Every time servants took a couple of steps the rope bridge swayed more than the last time.

I'll I could say to myself send me home now. I promise I will be a good girl from now on. I'll keep my bedroom clean and do my homework daily even if I'm unschooled Please!

At last, we all made it over the rope bridge and were on our way to see what was in store for us.

It was so rocky I was wondering what happened to the brown brick road sooner or later we would have to come to it again.

Going up the jagged rocks was hard for the servants who had to carry us in the Palanquin.

Could believe what I saw there were Trolls on the jagged rocks they were dressed like they were from the 1700s why would someone stick toy Trolls all over the rocks?

Out of the corner of my eyes, I saw one blinking and then one was walking, which must be my Imagination then all at once I heard a couple talking in a low screaky voice, now that was not my Imagination.

The queen looked around and looked at me "Do you trolls as well?

"At first, I thought it was just toy trolls until I saw one blinking then I kept saying it must be my imagining then I saw one walking and heard them talking then I knew they

were real."

A loud squeaky voice yelled, "Stop who goes there?"

When the four servants that were holding the Palanquin

Stopped and accidentally dropped the Palanquin and it went sliding down all the jagged rocks till we came to the bottom of the rocky hill.

The queen and I stepped out of the palanquin queen saw a big rip in the middle of the Palanquin.

With a huff, the Queen yelled"Here we go another mishap and delay this is taking us too long to get to the Emerald City!

"We can have one of the servants sew it up."

"I did not bring any pink thread. I didn't suspect anything like this to happen."

A small child troll came walking down the rocky hill and stood in front of The Queen. She held out her hand and in her right hand was pink thread and a needle.

"If you like I can sew up the hole ."

"That's very kind of you thank you."

The Queen ordered the servants to turn the Palanquin upside down so the hole could be sewed up.

The rest of the day she worked on sewing that hole and the next day too.

We were having a good time talking to them and telling the troll all our adventures and where we lived.

She just finished, but it was too dark for us to go on. We spent the night and the next morning the sun was up early and we started up the rocky hill once again this time we made it to the top. We waved goodbye and were on our way once.

Chapter 17

About an hour After leaving the trolls, I noticed there were broken pieces, of the brown brick road, The Queen and I both wondered what happened.

We came upon a ghost town that was like the ones you see in Western movies. It was kind of odd, I felt like someone was watching us, but I could not see anybody.

The Queen Bee was getting tired of just sitting, she wanted to get up and stretch her legs and find an outhouse.

"I need to use a bathroom. Darla said.

"Let's stop so we can all use the outhouse." The Queen Ordered.

As Darla got out she headed for the first building she saw.

"Where are you going, Darla?" The Queen asked.

"To the bathroom."

"You will not find a bathroom inside, this is a western ghost town, you need to use the outhouse."

Darla looked at The Queen with a strange look Darla was afraid to use an outhouse that had not been used in years. What if a rat came up when she was sitting on the toilet?

"What's wrong?"

"I'm afraid to use the outhouse, what if a rat comes up when I'm using the toilet?"

"You could just go right here in front of us all."

"I think I will use the outhouse if you do not mine."

It took us some tracking down to find one, but we did find one by the stables.

The Queen thought it might be a good idea if we stayed here and had lunch then moved on.

But I had the feeling we should have moved on now but it was not my call. I already messed it up by telling the Queen to take the brown brick road, when we should have taken the yellow brick road.

The servant was looking around as The Queen and I sat on the rocking chairs that were by the stable and mercantile and waited patiently for our lunch.

Some of the servants went in and found the food at the mercantile and it was still edible.

So it must not be too long ago people lived in this town. The servant brought out corn meal eggs, beef stakes, and potatoes to cook over the fire along with coffee and milk.

What a treat we never got beef steaks at home with 9 people living in a home, and with one other person living with us short term.

As lunch was being served I could hear someone walking on the other side of the building but couldn't make out who it was.

Along about then, a guy with gray hair and a gray beard turned the corner and he looked like a mountain man who was mining for gold.

"Well, I'll be I haven't seen anybody in town for a long time."

We just all looked at him before I spoke up "Hi, I'm Darla and this is The Queen Bee and her servants."

"It's nice to meet you all."

"I didn't get your name," Darla said

"I never told you, Hi, I'm Sam."

Sam looked over at the firepit where the servants were cooking.
"Have you eaten yet?" The Queen asked."
"Not today."

"Bring Sam a plate please." The queen ordered.

"Thanks"

We all sat around eating and talking to Sam I told him what happened to me and it was so fresh still," Darla said.

"This is where the witch's brother keeps his supply of food and you better watch out because he might have seen all of us eating his food you asked about the brown brick road, he thought if he had all servants break the brick road nobody would ever come this way."

"Let's get back in the Palanquin and get some sleep before the sun comes up Darla."

The sun came up and we packed up everything even the food that was left over from last night.

We said our goodbyes and once again we were on our way hoping this time we would be in Emerald City.

Chapter 18

It was a beautiful day and the sun was out and not too hot of a day. We went by lots of different farms but never ran into the wicked witch of the West bother.

I guess The Queen knew what she was talking about this was the wrong brick road to take.

I think sometimes I think I know it all but I'm only 7, I might as well just act my age.

The servant in the front of the line stopped without a warning and all the servants ran into each other, knocking each other down.

The Queen noticed on the hill that there was a cement castle and it looked dressy there was a dark cloud over the castle, but everywhere else the sky was blue without any clouds.

The Queen sneezed twice before she said a word "We better hurry up and get out of this area I think this might be the wicket witch of the West brother castle."

The servants got up and started walking faster than they had been walking.

But inside the castle Wicked Witch of the West's brother was asleep and didn't even know they were walking by.

AFTER SOME TIME THE castle was not in view and we felt better. We kept going just to make sure we were out of his sight.

Up ahead was a bright tall green building but there was a wooden fence it was the same color green as the building, Above the wooden door were some words but none of us could make them out because we were too far ahead

"I sure hope this is Elmeard City and not another road stop along the way I just want to get home."

"I'll we can do is move on to see if this is the Elmeard City."

It was about 12 minutes of walking before we got to the door, above the door was a sign that read Welcome to Elmeard City. on the right side was a bell to ring.

The servant at the head of the line rang the bell a minute later the door opened slowly a man was standing looking out at us.

"How can I help You?"

"The Queen Bee would like to speak Ozma if it is not too much of a problem."

"Where is The Queen Bee?"

"She over there sitting in the Palanquin."

"Can you have her come to the gate?"

"I'll go see if she will."

I turned around and headed in her direction. "Your Highness the person who opened the door would like to speak to you."

THE QUEENS STEPPED out of the Palanquin and walked up to the door.

"Why do you want to see Ozma?"

"I'm The Queen bee of Meadowfoam and my daughter wants to go back home to her human family."

"So your daughter a bee princess wants to go live with a human this does not make any sense."

I decided to do a condensed version of why we were coming to see The Queen "I found my daughter outside one night as a baby she still was too big for a beehive so I had to you some magic to make her small enough to fit in a beehive she stayed with me until she was 3 when she walked out of the hive, you know how toddlers are? She came back because she told me a bright light covered her and her brothers and sisters and she got caught in the part of the light that brought her back to me and she was the same size as she was the last time she lived with me.

I didn't want her to live but I told her I would take her to see Ozma in three days I was lying to her because I didn't want her to go back to the human family."

"Stop! You're giving me a headache. All go check and see if Ozma will see you wait here." the door slammed shut.

It seemed forever before the doorman came back. The door finally opened.

"Ozma will see you tomorrow you may come inside and camp by the door and I will come back tomorrow and get you."

The next day we were up early and sitting around waiting to see Ozma, the morning was almost over before the doorman came to get us, and as he started to approach us we all stood up.

"Please follow me and your servant can stay here nothing going to happen to them The Bee Queen I will make sure of it."

As we came into the glass building we saw a horse of many colors. "I guess I'm going to have to apologize to Larry I didn't believe him about the horse of many colors, everything else was just like Larry said, It was so pretty the brightest city I ever saw.

As we were heading to Ozma castle I saw the scarecrow walking our way. I couldn't believe I would be meeting one of my favorite characters in Oz.

"HI, it's nice to have you stop by we always like to see new people come to Emerald City." The Scrowcrow said.

happy to meet you." Darla said

Darla at first did not know what to say to them, she looked at the Scarecrow.

"I learned about you from Tammy."

The scarecrow noticed The Queen bee, "Long time no see."

"IT'S NICE TO SEE YOU once again."

The scarecrow noticed the wings on Darla scarecrow never saw a human bee, he looked at Darla.

"Who are you?"

"I'm Princes Darla."

The scarecrow explains having a puzzled look on his face like he did not understand.

The Queen noticed it right away, So once again she had to explain every then she noticed the scarecrow understood.

"Ozma would be delighted to see you all just follow me."

As they were walking up to the castle, Darla saw all the things her brother had told her about she was in ow at everything she saw, They made it to the castle door the scarecrow rang the bell before long one of the servants opened the door.

"What brings you here today the servant asked the scarecrow.

The scarecrow told the servant why Darla wanted to get back home to her human family.

"Well come on in and we will see what Ozma says."

It was a very long hallway before they got to the throne room, the servant rang the green bell to let Ozma know

that she had a visitor, and it took some time for Ozma to walk into the throne room.

"Nice to have you back scarecrow I have missed you."

"Likewise,"

Scarecrow explained everything The Bee told him.

"I see let me think about tell after we have dinner, and the band and dance are done with their performance."

Ozma rang the ball for the cook to come the cook ran into the throne room.

"We are having a party I want the best meal prepared."

"Yes, Your Highness." And the cook turns and leaves.

"Let me show our guest around the castle."

Almost every room had a different theme, one of the rooms was a rainbow room each wall was painted in the story of how Dorthy came to Oz and how she got to Emerald City.

Time went by fast Darla thought and the dinner bell rang.

Darla couldn't believe her eyes the table had more food than you see at the church on Thanksgiving.

They ate and talked. Darla enjoyed herself so much that for a second she thought it would be grand to live in Emerald City then her mind wandered back to her brothers and sisters and how much she missed them.

After dinner was done the band and dances came out and performed.

AFTER THE ENTERTAINMENT was over Ozma thanked them. "Go to the Kitchen and you can get your dinner."

Ozma looked at Dala, "I will send you back home to the human world but it is too late to get your ring the shop is closed now I will take you all to your bedroom for the night and then after breakfast, I will take you to the shop."

Before long morning and breakfast were over and they were all on their way to the jewelry store.

Ozma walked in first, Then The Queen, and then Darla the scarecrow was the last one to walk into the store.

"Good day, Ozma how can I help you?"

"I need one ring that can send Dala home and back to visit."

"I will be right back with the ring."

"Now Darla you have to remember to never take the ring off or let anybody else try it on or you will never be able to come back here and visit anybody."

He came back with a lovely ring and handed it to Ozma.

"Put your right hand out Darla and Ozma placed the ring on her fourth finger.

"Let's go out of the shop Ozma told Darla all you have to do is turn the ring twice and say these words I want to go back and visit The Queen Bee, if you want to visit me say send me to Emerald City. Now say your goodbyes and I will tell you what you must say to get home.

Darla had tears in her eyes she enjoyed herself most of the time, but she knew she had to get back home, so she hugged every.

"I'm ready to be sent home."

" Turn your ring twice and say these words. "Sent me back to where I was before I went into the beehive.

Before Darla said a word she took one more look around Emerald City.

Darla turned her ring twice and said. "Send me back to where I was before I went into the beehive."

In no time flat Dala was back standing by her brothers and sisters on the road heading back home.

Also by Josie Ann Tyler

Family of Oz series
Jigsaw Puzzle of Oz
Hairdresser Of Oz
Meadowfoam of Oz

Standalone
Kingdome Blown To Unknown Part Of Oz
Farmer Boy Of Oz The First Book In The Family Of Oz series